GRETEL KILLEEN

My Sister's a
Sea Slug

Illustrated by Zeke and Eppie

from Zeke, Eppie and Gretel

MY SISTER'S A SEA SLUG
A RED FOX BOOK 0 09 944807 6

Published in Great Britain by Red Fox,
an imprint of Random House Children's Books

PRINTING HISTORY
First published in Australia by Random House Australia Pty Ltd, 1999
Red Fox edition published, 2003

1 3 5 7 9 10 8 6 4 2

Red Fox books are published by Random House Children's Books,
61–63 Uxbridge Road, London W5 5SA,
a division of The Random House Group Ltd,
in Australia by Random House Australia (Pty) Ltd,
20 Alfred Street, Milsons Point, Sydney, NSW 2061, Australia,
in New Zealand by Random House New Zealand Ltd,
18 Poland Road, Glenfield, Auckland 10, New Zealand,
and in South Africa by Random House (Pty) Ltd,
Endulini, 5A Jubilee Road, Parktown 2193, South Africa

THE RANDOM HOUSE GROUP Limited Reg. No. 954009

A CIP catalogue record for this book is available from the British Library.

Printed and bound in Great Britain by Clays Ltd, St Ives plc

www.kidsatrandomhouse.co.uk

The Random House Group Limited supports The Forest Stewardship
Council® (FSC®), the leading international forest-certification organisation.
Our books carrying the FSC label are printed on FSC®-certified paper.
FSC is the only forest-certification scheme supported by the leading
environmental organisations, including Greenpeace. Our
paper procurement policy can be found at
www.randomhouse.co.uk/environment